One day, Rabbit
was feeling bored.
"I wish **something** would happen,"
he said.

"Excuse me,"

said a voice. "May I help?"

It was Wolf.

"Well, maybe . . . " said Rabbit. "I'm **bored.**"

"Why don't we write a story?"
said Wolf. "I am a **librarian**, you know,
and librarians know a **lot**
about stories."

"You don't **look** like a librarian," said Rabbit.
"What **big ears** you've got!"

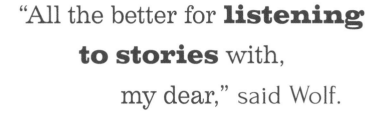

"All the better for **listening to stories** with, my dear," said Wolf.

"And what **big eyes** you've got!" said Rabbit.

"All the better for **reading** with, my dear," said Wolf.

"Hmmm, I'm sure I've heard something like that before," said Rabbit.

"Never mind that," said Wolf quickly.
"Let's get on with the story."

"But how do we start?"
asked Rabbit.

"You need to
USE YOUR IMAGINATION!
It's making up *words* and pictures in your head to tell a story," explained Wolf. "And, of course, there's really only **one** way to begin a story . . .

"But **what** is our story going to be about?"
asked Rabbit.

"Well," said Wolf. **"USE YOUR IMAGINATION."**

"Space rockets!" cried Rabbit. "BIG explosions!!
And bananas. We need LOTS of bananas!!!"

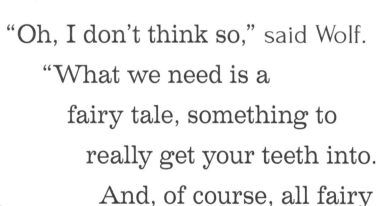

"Oh, I don't think so," said Wolf.
"What we need is a
fairy tale, something to
really get your teeth into.
And, of course, all fairy tales
need a baddie."

"What about a mouse?"
asked Rabbit.

"I was thinking about
something **bigger,**"
said Wolf.

"An **elephant!**" cried Rabbit.

"How about something
medium-sized?"
said Wolf, quickly.

"I know! What about **you?**"
asked Rabbit.

"Now, **that's**
a good idea,"
said Wolf.

"What next?" asked Rabbit.

"Well, of course, we need a hero," said Wolf.

"Me, me, me!" said Rabbit.

"What a great idea!" said Wolf.

"But what will I wear?" said Rabbit.

"Oh, it doesn't matter much," said Wolf. **"USE YOUR IMAGINATION."**

"A **SPACE SUIT!**" cried Rabbit.
"Or a **pirate's hat!**
Or . . . what about a little red cape?"

"Oh, you probably
don't need a thing,"
smiled Wolf.

"But where does this story happen?" asked Rabbit.

"USE YOUR IMAGINATION," said Wolf.

"That's a tricky one," said Rabbit.
"What do **you** think?"

"I was thinking of somewhere . . . tree-y," said Wolf.

"Oh, what about a **forest?**" squeaked Rabbit.

"Now, that's a good idea," said Wolf.

Rabbit felt very proud. "We've got a baddie, a hero
AND a forest," he said. "Is the story going to start soon?"

"Oh, yes," said Wolf, grinning. "The story starts . . .

. . . RIGHT NOW!"

"I don't like this story **at all!**" panted Rabbit...

as Wolf

chased after

him.

"Really?" snarled Wolf.
"Well, don't worry.
We're nearly
at the
end."

"I don't think so,"
said Rabbit, suddenly stopping.
"I'm the hero, after all . . .
and I'm going to

USE MY IMAGINATION!"

And so . . .

. . . Rabbit did.

"This *isn't* a good
idea **AT ALL,**"
said Wolf.

"Really?" grinned Rabbit.
"Well, don't worry,
we're nearly
at the **end."**

5, 4, 3, 2, 1 . . .

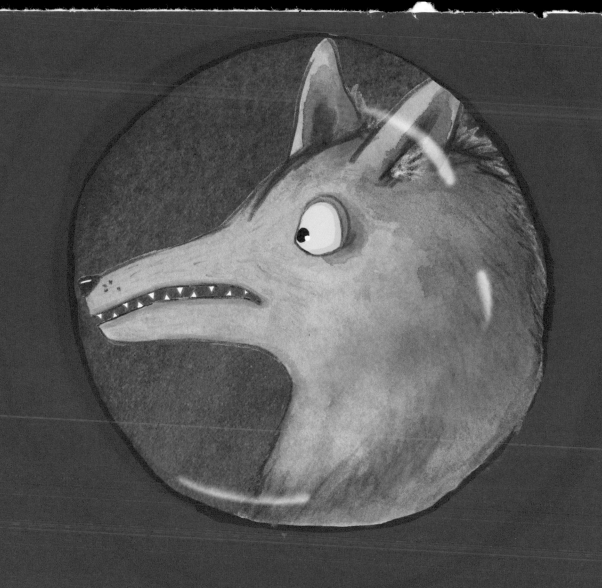

LIFT
UP

AST
FF!

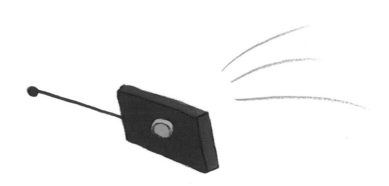

"Now **that** was
a good idea,"
said Rabbit . . .

"Isn't **IMAGINATION** a wonderful thing?"